Missy President

WRITTEN BY RANDI ZUCKERBERG
WITH NATASHA LEWIN
ILLUSTRATED BY JOAN COLEMAN

Missy President by Randi Zuckerberg & Natasha Lewin

Published by: Zuckerberg Ink, LLC

Illustrated by: Joan Coleman / www.InkWonderland.com

ISBN: 978-0-692-79484-5
LCCN: 2016917294

First Edition, October 2016
10 9 8 7 6 5 4 3 2 1

Published in New York City
Printed in the U.S.A

iPod is a trademark of Apple Inc.

Books may be purchased in bulk quantity with discounted pricing by contacting the publisher, Zuckerberg Ink, at Park West Finance Station, P.O. Box 20900, New York, NY 10025; or by email at sales@zuckerbergmedia.com.

NOTE FROM THE AUTHOR

Missy 1.0

To voters big and small,

As a mom, I've struggled to find a way to talk to my kids about this particular election season. And as a technologist, I've spent years encouraging kids to be good digital citizens. When I put my thoughts and feelings on both subjects together, *Missy President* was born.

Folks in the publishing industry know that illustrated books can take years to develop. Thanks to new technology (and a fantastic team) we were able to bring Missy to life in a matter of weeks. While we're excited that Missy could enter the world when the world seems to need her most, we also acknowledge that her story is a work in progress. And Missy will only ever become everything she can become if you let me know how she can improve.

So here's my proposition to you:

Tell me what you think! Whether via our website, over social media or by email, I'd love to know what you like and dislike about Missy. Tell me what you think of where her journey has taken her so far, and what you hope to see her accomplish in the future.

And as a special thank-you for supporting our early efforts, now through Election Day 2016, for every re-tweet of *Missy President* social media posts, <u>I will donate one copy to an underserved school or library.</u> For more information, please follow us on Facebook and Twitter @Missy4Prez and use the hashtag #MissyPresident when you post.

Do we have a deal? Together, we'll add a little joy to this political season - and maybe even inspire a future leader or two in the process.

Love,
RZ

This book is for my sons, Asher and Simi, and for all the awesome women they will work for.

-RANDI ZUCKERBERG

For my niece, Natalie, who has endless possibilities at her fingertips and love for all the world in her heart.

-NATASHA LEWIN

CHAPTER 1

Missy looked down at her notebook. She'd been working on her school assignment for over an hour, and the only thing she had to show for it was one line, "If I Were President," scrawled in messy handwriting across the top of the page.

Missy's fourth grade teacher, Mr. Armas, had assigned everyone in the class to write a speech about what they would do if they were President of the United States. Missy was stuck.

"Ugh," she groaned, ripping the page out of her notebook, crumpling it, and tossing it in the air toward the trash can.

"UGH!" she groaned more loudly as the paper narrowly missed the trash can.

She never missed a shot! In fact, her nickname on the school basketball team was "Never Miss Missy."

As if on cue, Missy's mom entered the living room with some healthy snacks and a glass of Missy's favorite lemonade. "How's your speech going, Missy?"

"It's not," Missy pouted, pulling on one of her red curls. "Why is my homework never about sports? Or Wonder Woman? Or frogs? I know plenty about those things."

"I think this is a great assignment, Missy!" her mom enthused. "The election is coming up next week, and I think it's wonderful that Mr. Armas is getting your class excited and involved. You can't vote in this election, but you will one day!"

"Fine. I'll try again," Missy said, lowering her pen to her notebook. "What would I do as President of the United States? Hmmm... hmmm... UGH!" Missy dropped her pen in frustration. "I got nothing. Mom, why does everything sound so much better when I'm thinking it?!"

Mom gave Missy a supportive pat on the head. "Honey, before you write anything down, why don't you try just saying it out loud to me? From the heart?"

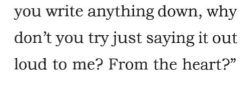

At that moment, Missy's older sister Gloria sauntered into the room, clad in all the latest fashion styles. She had headphones on, and was carrying a smartphone, an iPod, and a tablet. Missy thought that Gloria must be the coolest 13-year-old on Earth.

"Oh, good, Gloria—you're just in time," Mom said. But Gloria didn't hear. She was too busy rocking out with her headphones. *"Gloria, I'm talking to you!"* Mom said a bit more loudly. When Gloria still didn't respond, Mom gently pulled one of the headphones out of her ear, and then seemed puzzled when she realized there wasn't actually any music playing. "You weren't even listening to anything!" Mom exclaimed.

"I know," Gloria said nonchalantly, "but it's a good way to ignore people if they *think* you're listening to something."

Mom gave an exasperated sigh. "Well, young lady, enough with the ignoring act. You're just in time to hear Missy tell us what she would do as president."

"Ha!" Gloria snorted. "That's a laugh. Missy? President? As *if.*"

"If I were president, I would send Gloria away to Canada. There, I'm done," Missy growled.

"Enough, you two," Mom said sternly. "Gloria, sit down. Missy, tell us why we should vote for you for president on Tuesday."

"Fine," Gloria said, sitting down in a huff next to her mother on the sofa.

"Fine!" Missy said, defeated, and then stood up in front of them.

She took a deep breath. "If I were President of—"

"Wait!" Gloria said, holding up her phone. "You need the perfect presidential outfit for this speech." She opened up a photo app that placed a red, white, and blue top hat on Missy in real time. "There you go," she said, showing the phone to Missy. "Much more presidential."

"That looks dumb," Missy pouted, crossing her arms. "I don't want to do this in front of Gloria if she's going to be that way."

"Gloria..." Mom turned to her older daughter with a sharp glance. "No more distracting Missy from her homework. Okay, Missy, let's try again."

Missy took a deep breath. Gloria pretended to put her phone away, but she secretly turned it to video and started recording Missy, unbeknownst to both her and Mom.

"Hi, my name is Missy. I think America is the best country on Earth. Even the entire solar system! Although Uranus is pretty funny—but that's beside the point. I love America, especially the great American pastime of baseball! But when it comes to politics? BORING. Everyone talks about the political parties. But there's nothing about either of them that sounds like a party to me. How about the Slumber Party? Now *that's* a party I could get behind. Both of these not-really-a-party parties spend so much time talking about what's wrong with our country. I just wish that everyone could remember how awesome this place is and get as excited about America as I am!"

Missy did a cartwheel and continued her speech, so carried away by her excitement that she was almost in a trance-like state. Gloria chuckled to herself, still filming the video gold.

"Every day should be like the Fourth of July!" Missy exclaimed, making firework noises. "BOOM! BOOM! *Crackle! Fizz!* We need more holidays celebrating how great our nation is! We need to always be friendly and love and respect one another!

"If I were president I'd hold karaoke press conferences, design Oval Office obstacle courses, and create more jobs by building a year-round carnival on the White House lawn! There'd be a Ferris wheel and cotton candy and even a few clowns. But not the *scary* kind of clowns—the good kind."

Missy was still dancing around the living room. "And that's another thing the White House needs—COLOR! I'd paint the White House a thousand different colors to represent the different kinds of people who live all around the country and come here from all over the world!"

At this point, Missy began tearing pieces of her notebook into confetti and throwing them so that they rained down all over her and the room. "I'd create new national holidays like *Say Hi to Your Neighbor Day* and *Pull Your Pants Way, Way Up Day*—and I'd rename the whole month of August *Dog-gust*, because every parent would be required to get their kids a new puppy!"

Missy looked straight at Mom and Gloria with her fist held high. "These ideas are for you. For US! Instead of arguing over America's rules, let's celebrate the fact that *America rules*! This is Missy President, and I approve this message."

Nobody spoke for a few seconds.

Then Gloria rolled her eyes. "Don't be such a dope."

"*I am not a dope!*" Missy declared.

Gloria pressed stop on her video and stuck the phone in her pocket. "Mom, can I go back to my room now?"

Mom ignored the question. "Missy, that was fantastic! What a wonderful imagination you have. If you can capture even half of that enthusiasm on paper, Mr. Armas is going to love your assignment."

"Thanks, Mom," Missy beamed. "You and Dad would make awesome First Parents! Speaking of how awesome you are, how about a super-duper awesome trip to go get some froyo?"

"Nice try, Missy, but you have some homework to do," Mom laughed. "I'll be in the study if you need me."

Gloria smirked as she walked back to her room. "Let's see what the Internet has to say about this one," she said to herself as she uploaded the video. "I'll title it *Missy President.*"

CHAPTER 2

About an hour later, Missy, Gloria, and their parents were all sitting at the dinner table. It wasn't an especially peaceful dinner, though. Phones kept ringing off the hook. The home phone, Gloria's phone, Dad's work phone—all were ringing like crazy.

Ring... ring... rrring...

"MOM—can I PUH-LEEZ answer it?" Gloria begged.

Ring... ring... rrrring...

"Honey, I really should answer this call," Dad chimed in.

"Both of you know that we have a strict no-phones-at-the-dinner-table policy," Mom replied sternly.

"When everyone is finished and we've cleaned up, then you can go back to your phone calls and texting and Snap-whatevers. But until then, you *sit!*"

Dad and Gloria began shoveling food into their mouths as quickly as possible, so they could return to their phones. On the other side of the table, Missy was eating as slowly as she could to avoid going back to her homework. She was down to eating one pea at a time from the pile on her plate.

Gloria kicked her under the table.

"OW!" Missy exclaimed.

"Are you okay, Missy? Should I call a doctor?" Dad asked, reaching eagerly for his phone.

"NO PHONES!" Mom said angrily, grabbing it out of his hand.

"Eat faster!" Gloria whispered angrily. When Missy instead continued eating one pea at a time, Gloria leaned in closer. "Fine. What's it going to take? My dessert?"

Ring... ring.... rrrrring....

Gloria bit her lip in frustration as her phone rang yet again. "Okay. How about my dessert for a whole week?"

Missy's eyes lit up. "Deal." And with that, she picked up her plate, tipped it against her mouth, and downed all her peas in one gulp. "Done!"

Gloria and Dad raced their plates to the dishwasher and vanished from the room so fast that the rest of the dishes on the table spun.

"Who could be calling at this time of night that's so important?" Mom wondered out loud.

"Why do we have a landline, and how do people know the number for it?" Missy also wondered out loud.

"Well, Missy, it looks like it's just you and me for dessert tonight," Mom said as Missy helped her clear the table. "And thank you for being so helpful with the dishes, even though I know it's only to keep from doing your homework. I'll tell you what: you go finish your assignment, and then we'll go get that frozen yogurt you mentioned. I know it's your favorite."

Mom had said the magic words! As Missy turned to leave the kitchen, both Gloria and Dad screamed: "AAAGH!"

Mom panicked. "Gloria? Honey? What's wrong?"

"AAAAAGH!" Gloria and Dad screamed again in unison, both still on their phones as they ran back to the kitchen.

"It's Missy!" Dad exclaimed breathlessly. "She's all over the Internet talking about being president."

"But how?" Mom asked incredulously.

"Huh?" said Missy, confused.

"I can't believe it. Missy's *famous*. That silly video I—"

Gloria clapped her hand over her mouth as soon as she realized what she'd said.

"Gloria! YOU did this?" Mom turned to her, glaring.

"Ummm... well... I was just so proud of Missy with her speech, and I wanted more people to see it and... umm..." Gloria had been caught red-handed. "I was bored, and *you* made me watch it!"

"Gloria, take it down this instant!"

"I *can't*, Mom. The Internet doesn't work that way. Once it's out there, it's *out* there."

"Okay, well, how many people have watched it? Surely it can't be *that* many. I mean, we were just seeing this speech ourselves," Mom said hopefully.

"Millions," Dad said, shaking his head. "Millions of people have watched this video. It's everywhere. It's *viral.*"

"Hashtag Internet Broken," Gloria deadpanned. Nobody laughed.

Suddenly, Missy felt ill. The room started spinning. She sat down on the floor. "*Millions* of people? I'm *viral*? I think I *feel* viral."

"Gloria, you shouldn't have uploaded this video without

Missy's—and definitely not without *our*—permission first," Dad scolded.

"Until you learn how to use a smartphone responsibly, you're going to be without one," Mom said. "Hand it over right now." Gloria sadly gave over her phone to her parents.

Missy left, despondently walking back to her bedroom, right across from the #KEEPOUTMISSY sign that hung on Gloria's door. Missy crawled into her bed and fell asleep, hoping this would all turn out to be one big, bad dream.

CHAPTER 3

Missy woke up bright and early the next morning. Everything in her room seemed normal. "Phew! It was just a bad dream," she thought, pulling on a baseball jersey, jeans, and sneakers for another *awesome* day of school.

But when she pulled up her window shade, a hundred flashbulbs went off, and she saw crowds of people standing on the street at the foot of her driveway. She quickly pulled the shade down and went running into the living room. "Mom? Dad? Gloria? What's going on?"

The usual morning quiet on Missy's street had been interrupted by dozens of news vans lining the block, reporters with microphones held high, cameramen with wide-range equipment, and plenty of nosy neighbors, all hoping to catch a glimpse of the now-famous girl who had big ideas for America: Missy President.

Peering out from the various windows in her house, Missy saw people with signs parading by. The signs read, "MISSY PUTS THE FUN BACK IN FUNDING" and "AMERICA RULES, NOT AMERICA'S RULES" and "MISSY, GO HOME."

"But I *am* home," Missy said, scratching her head.

Mom, Dad, and Gloria were all gathered around the TV.

"*Missy President* is now at 160 million views, and the number is expected to rise as the day goes on," said the news anchor, as Gloria's recording of Missy appeared on TV. Missy watched herself proclaiming, "I just wish that everyone could remember how awesome this place is and get as excited about America as I am!"

Realizing that Missy was in the room, Mom quickly changed the channel. But this new channel was covering the *Missy President* phenomena as well. "Excuse me, sir," a reporter asked a jogger running by on the street. "Have you seen the *Missy President* video?"

"Seen it? I *live* it!" the man said, ripping off his jogging jacket to reveal a T-shirt with Missy's face on it. The T-shirt read, "I AM NOT A DOPE!"

"She has something that none of the other candidates have," the man said, a little out of breath from his jog. "She's not a dope!"

"I really wish you'd cut that part out, Gloria," Mom sighed.

"How did they get shirts printed that quickly?" Dad wondered.

"I should have thought of that," Gloria huffed, walking over to the window and peering through the curtain. "That's a *lot* of cameras. Wow."

"But why are they all here?" Missy said in a small, choked voice.

"They're fascinated by you!" Dad exclaimed. "You're the first fresh, new thing they've had to talk about in this entire election cycle! They *love* you!"

"We love you!" Mom said, blowing a kiss to Missy on TV.

"But they don't even *know* me," Missy said.

"But, boy, do they want to," Dad replied. "CNN called. *Sesame Street* called. It's been a madhouse, and it's not even 9 a.m.!"

Back on television, a female news anchor chimed in: "Even as I speak, the startling number of views for *Missy President* is skyrocketing. Let's go to Harry, live on the streets of Atlanta."

The screen flashed to an older man in a suit jacket. "Diane, I've talked to everyone out here, and every single one of 'em has seen Missy's speech. Some have even memorized it!"

"Memorized it? Could they hand in my homework for me?" Missy said, suddenly realizing that she'd never actually finished her assignment *on paper*.

"C'mon, girls, enough of this—it's time for school!" Mom said, abruptly turning off the TV and gathering up their backpacks. "Meet me at the front door in five minutes."

"But all those reporters! I need at least fifteen minutes to do my makeup," Gloria said.

"No makeup for school—you're thirteen years old!" Mom snapped. "Front door. Five minutes."

"I don't want to go out there in front of all those reporters," Missy said.

"I have an idea," Mom replied, digging through the coat closet and pulling out a bunch of trench coats and sunglasses.

"You mean, like, *disguises*?" Missy lit up.

"Cool!" Gloria said. Then, realizing that Missy also liked the idea, she quickly changed it to: "I mean, ugh! How *lame*."

A few minutes later, Missy, Mom, and Dad, wearing trench coats, sunglasses, and hats, all sprinted out of the house toward the car. Gloria followed behind, strutting as if on a runway, all dolled up for the cameras.

The reporters weren't fooled. They swarmed around the family as they rushed to the car, shoving cameras and microphones in Missy's face, asking questions all at once.

"Missy, what party are you registered with? Rumor has it you're starting the Birthday Party?"

"Missy, who have you picked as vice president?"

"What's your platform?"

"Who are you wearing?"

"Missy, Gloria, get in the car!" Dad ushered the girls in and then jumped in himself, as Mom started the car and quickly reversed down the driveway, with the reporters shouting after Missy and taking photo after photo after photo after photo after...

CHAPTER 4

...photo after photo.

They drove down Main Street, past Hello Deli, past Timmy O'Toole's Hardware Store. Nobody spoke. The entire family was in shock.

Mom switched on the radio.

A radio deejay with a thick Southern drawl was saying, "Y'all, everybody down here in Texas just *looooves* that little Missy girl."

Mom changed the station.

A church announcer was saying, "...and a voice from the heavens told me, 'Watcheth Missy's video.' So I did. And it was good!"

Missy's mom turned the radio off as quickly as she'd turned it on.

"Silence is good, too," Dad agreed.

All the way down to Amelia Earhart Elementary School they drove, with news vans, reporters, and fans following every inch of the way, all wanting to catch a quick glimpse of Missy President. Mom stopped the car in the school's parking lot as the reporters crowded around them.

"Okay, we all run in on the count of *three*," Mom said. "One, two... *three!*" Missy, Gloria, Mom, and Dad opened their doors and ran for the front entrance of the school.

The reporters tried to keep up, but Mr. Armas was there, gesturing wildly from his wheelchair, instructing two security guards to keep the reporters at bay.

"Hurry!" Mr. Armas said, holding the doors open wide for Missy and her family. Once inside, they all had to catch their breath. "That sure was close," Mr. Armas said, wiping the sweat from his forehead.

"Mr. Armas," Missy began. "I actually didn't even get a chance to do my homework. But even without doing it, I went viral. Which sounds really scary but apparently just means that, like, 200 million people watched my video. Which, when you think of it, really is scary. But—

"Missy," said Mr. Armas, interrupting her. "Are you okay? That's what's most important here."

"This is coo-coo crazy pants," Missy said softly, staring down at her tennis shoes.

"Well, don't you worry about the assignment," Mr. Armas said, putting a hand on her shoulder. "You *aced* it—A+++. Even better, Principal Laing asked if you could talk at the school assembly today. The entire country wants to hear from Missy President, and we have you right here in this school. What do you say, Missy?"

"I don't know," Missy said, suddenly feeling a bit *viral* again. "I'm not much of a public speaker. I don't really like getting up in front of people."

"Well, you sure could have fooled me with that video," Mr. Armas said. "You did a great thing, Missy—you inspired *millions* of people. You made them feel excited about our country again. I think it would be wonderful for the school to hear your message."

"I'm pretty sure they already have," Gloria mumbled under her breath.

Dad shot Gloria a warning look.

"You can do this, Missy. You're smart and strong and super-brave," Mom said.

Missy smiled for the first time that morning. "Okay, Mr. Armas—I'll do it."

"Amazing!" Dad said. "I'll call the salon to reschedule my clients."

"And I'll call my assistant to reschedule my meetings," Mom chimed in.

"And I'll go to the nurse and pretend I'm sick, so I can miss the assembly," Gloria muttered.

"It's settled then," Mr. Armas grinned excitedly. "I'll tell Principal Laing that it's a go. Missy, you're on at noon!"

As her fourth-grade teacher wheeled off, and her parents pulled out their phones to rearrange their schedules, Missy tried to put on her bravest, most excited face. But she really wasn't feeling very excited at all.

CHAPTER 5

A few hours later, the gymnasium was packed with students, teachers, camera crews, and reporters. A lone microphone stood in the middle of the basketball court with a sign reading, "MISSY PRESIDENT." Missy stood in the corner, biting her nails nervously.

"What's wrong, Missy? Stage fright?" Mr. Armas asked.

"Oh, Mr. Armas, I don't know what to say to all these people. What if I let them down?"

"Let them down? They love you because you spoke from the heart. You said wonderful things about this great nation that reflected the thoughts that most U.S. citizens have. They only want to hear *more* from you. You'll do great," Mr. Armas said encouragingly as Principal Laing stepped up to the microphone. "Okay, it's time."

The audience went crazy, with shouts of "WOOO! HOORAY! YEE-HAW! WOOT! WE WANT MISSY! *MISSY! MISSY! MISSY!*"

"I didn't think anyone in this school even knew who I was," Missy whispered to Mr. Armas.

Principal Laing managed to quiet the crowd down. "Yes, yes—go Missy! Good afternoon, students. It's me, Principal Laing of Amelia Earhart Elementary. I hope you're all having a great day today."

"I AM NOT A DOPE!" someone screamed from the back of the crowd. The audience erupted in laughter and cheers.

"Exactly—me neither," said Principal Laing, "which is why I've asked Missy, a fourth-grader at our school—who is now probably the most famous fourth-grader in the whole country—to talk to all of us today so that we can all hear her inspiring message together. Without further delay, I give you the little lady of the hour, Missy President!"

Missy walked out slowly to the microphone, looking around at all the cheering, screaming faces. Twenty-four hours ago, she was basically invisible. And now here she was, standing next to the principal, about to give a speech about a video that pretty much the entire country had seen. *Yikes!* Principal Laing made way for Missy at the microphone as the crowd cheered her on.

"MISSY, MISSY, MISSY—"

Missy cleared her throat. "I, umm... I didn't really have a speech planned or anything. But I guess that, uh, well, most of you have sort of already seen my other speech."

Missy paused and glanced over at Mom, who gave her an encouraging glance.

"Thank you, everyone, for watching my video," Missy continued. From the front row, Gloria stamped her foot and coughed.

"I guess now that, um, *our* video got your attention and stuff," Missy continued, not wishing to make Gloria feel bad, "I'd like to talk about something especially important happening in America tomorrow, actually—um, the presidential election."

The news cameras zoomed in on her. "Missy, who are you voting for?" one of the reporters called out.

"Um, well, I'm only in fourth grade, so I can't legally vote," Missy replied.

"Oh, right. Interesting..." the reporter said, frantically scribbling in his notepad.

"I know most of us in this gym aren't old enough to vote," Missy continued, "but there are some of you here that are. Like my mom and dad, and Mr. Armas, and Principal Laing, and all the teachers, and anyone else who watches this on TV. Or the Internet! Because with all the phones I see pointed in my direction, I guess this speech will be up there pretty soon." Missy shot a quick glance at Gloria who was pouting in her seat, unable to record Missy with her phone like so many of her peers around her.

"One thing that's easy to forget," Missy said, "is that most people in this country didn't always have the right to vote. A lot of people had to fight to get it. Like, fight really, *really* hard. They did it for us, so that every gender, race, religion, and creed could have an equal say in what's best for America. So if you can, be sure to cast your vote for president tomorrow—no matter who it is that you choose." Pausing for a second, she surveyed the crowd. "DON'T BE A DOPE—VOTE!" she yelled.

The crowd went wild as everyone leaped to their feet to give Missy a standing ovation. Missy bowed quickly and ran off the stage. Mr. Armas and her family rushed to her side.

"I'm so proud of you!" Mom gushed.

"You've sure got a way with words," Dad said lovingly.

"Great job, Missy!" Mr. Armas added.

Everyone looked at Gloria, who just rolled her eyes, gesturing to Missy. "It wasn't *terrible*," she finally admitted.

"Coming from Gloria, that's high praise," Dad chuckled.

CHAPTER 6

ELECTION DAY

The late morning sun peeked in behind the curtains of Missy's messy bedroom. She blinked her eyes open and looked at her alarm clock to see—WHAT?! 11:59 a.m.?! How could that be? How could she have overslept when she had to be at school?

Missy bounded out of bed, tripping over dirty laundry, baseballs and tennis balls, her pet frog Trog's cage, books on frogs, and an assortment of sneakers and sports equipment covering every inch of the floor.

"I really need to clean this place," Missy muttered. "But not today, because I am super-*duper* late. Yikes!"

Not even noticing that she was wearing two different shoes, her pants the wrong way, and her shirt inside out, Missy raced into the living room, all set to apologize profusely and ask why nobody had bothered to wake her up.

But she stopped when she saw Mom, Dad, and Gloria with their mouths wide open and their eyes popping out of their heads like three cartoon characters as they all listened to a reporter on TV.

"In a shocking turn of events, voters in record numbers are writing in Missy for president on their official ballots. Her *Don't be a Dope—Vote* speech is blowing this election out of the water," the reporter said.

"What happened?" Missy asked.

"*You* happened," Dad replied.

"Oh, no! *Still?*" Missy groaned. "But I'm not even running."

"Voters can write in anyone that's not on the ballot for the presidential election," Dad replied.

"Yeah, last year Mickey Mouse was written in by eleven people," Gloria volunteered.

"And this year, people are writing your name in record numbers," Mom said. "Look!" She changed the channel to a thin blonde woman and a tall dark-haired man having a debate.

"Missy's entry into this race shouldn't really shock anyone since your candidate is such a lousy, crooked liar," the woman said.

"Didn't your candidate ask a restaurant if they had bald eagle on the menu? How much lower could he possibly stoop?" the man replied angrily.

Mom changed the channel again to a female talk show host jumping up and down on a sofa.

"YOU get a new president! And YOU get a new president! And YOU get a new president!" the host declared enthusiastically as the entire audience cheered.

Mom changed the channel again. A silver-fox TV anchor was saying, "Very early exit polls show Missy as a real contender..."

Mom changed the channel again, this time to a home decorating show.

"...and since the Oval Office lacks corners, I think this curved monkey-shaped shelving unit with a built-in slide would be just what Missy needs to spice up the geometry of the room."

"Everyone is talking about you, Missy!" Mom said, half in disbelief, half in excitement. She changed the channel again and landed on a group of five women sitting around a table.

"Missy can't take office! She's only nine years old! She should be outside building tree forts or something!" one woman said.

"Didn't you hear? Nine is the new thirty-five!" another woman responded.

"Does anybody even *build* tree forts anymore?" a third woman asked. "I mean, doesn't that comment sort of discriminate against people who live in apartment buildings?"

As a fight ensued among the five women, Mom quickly changed the channel back to the silver-fox TV anchor. "We only have the numbers for the East Coast coming in now," he said.

"Maybe the West Coast will be smarter," Gloria quipped.

"But no matter what part of the country you're in," the anchor continued, "it's clear that the American public wants Missy to be the next president of our United States."

"Mom? Could I actually *be* president?" Missy asked quietly.

"One day? Sure. But not while you're living under this roof," Mom replied, turning the TV off. "I'm sorry, Missy—I know all the things they're saying on television are exciting, but it wouldn't even be *possible* for you to become president. You're too young. You're nine years old! You're just a kid." Turning to Dad, Mom gave him a look and said, "Back me up here!"

"Uh... I... um..." Dad stumbled. "Is it even legal anyway? Who can tell?"

At that precise moment, the doorbell rang. Missy ran to open it.

"DON'T OPEN THE DOOR!" Mom and Dad shouted at the exact same time.

Missy peered through the keyhole and saw a familiar face. "It's Mr. Armas!"

"Okay, Missy, back away from the door—I'll handle this. It might be someone *pretending* to be Mr. Armas," Dad said, taking himself very seriously.

"O... kay," Missy said, wondering if her parents had lost it.

"Missy, it's Mr. Armas!" Dad called out moments later.

"I *know* that," Missy mumbled to herself. "Hi, Mr. Armas!" she called out warmly, helping to wheel her fourth-grade teacher into the living room. Mr. Armas had a big grin on his face and a huge pile of books on his lap. "Tough getting through that crowd outside," he said. "Someone asked me if I was Missy's military strategist!

"But never mind all that," Mr. Armas continued. "Missy, you're one step away from becoming president! I always knew my fourth-graders would go on to do great things, but I never imagined it would happen while they were *still* in fourth grade!"

"But Mom said it's not possible," Missy replied.

"She's probably right," Mr. Armas said. "That's why I brought these books. There might be a loophole in here somewhere, and if there is, we'll find it." He began passing the books around. "Everyone gets one."

Gloria rolled her eyes. "Sorry—not in school, not reading books," she said, leaving the room.

"I brought the Constitution, the Declaration of Independence, and *Being President for Dummies*," Mr. Armas said, handing out books.

"I'll take that last one," Dad said.

"We only have a few hours before they call the election, so let's get started," Mr. Armas announced in full-on teacher mode. "Remember, everyone, we're looking for a clause that would allow a nine-year-old to take office."

Mom scowled. "Fine. I'll help because I'm curious—but even if we do find something, I won't allow Missy to be president. Not under this roof," she reminded everyone, as they cracked the books open and began their race against the clock.

"Go Team Missy President!" Mr. Armas said, as everyone dug in.

CHAPTER 7

Missy, Mom, Dad, and Mr. Armas scoured their books for hours, as Gloria switched between sitting in her room staring at the ceiling, sitting on the sofa watching the news reports with Missy's name rising in the polls, and generally pacing around the living room saying things like, "Too bad, so sad," secretly wanting to help but not wanting to admit it.

Missy stroked her pet frog, Trog, in her lap, hoping he would help her think. Dad wiped the sweat from his forehead with a handkerchief. Mr. Armas chewed on a pencil. It was getting down to the wire and, still, nothing—not even a *hint* of something. Missy even tried doing a headstand and reading the Constitution upside down to see if that sparked an idea, but nada.

"I got it!" Mom said, suddenly standing up with her fist clenched.

Everyone looked at her excitedly.

"Oh, sorry," Mom said. "I meant I got the fly that's been buzzing around this room for the past hour." She fed the captured fly to Trog, who croaked happily, and then returned to her book.

"It's useless, Mr. Armas!" Missy groaned. "Nothing in these books says anything about how a nine-year-old can be president. Let's just give up!" She flopped to the floor, defeated, as Gloria changed the channel to a reporter announcing the latest polls.

"Currently, the runner-up has only seven votes—which is strange because he has at least *eight* voting-age family members. Despite the fact that it seems like even members of his *own family* voted for Missy, he's still the runner-up, which means that unless Missy figures out a way to fight the age restriction, he'll be our new president," the reporter said.

That's when a light bulb went off for Mr. Armas.

"Eureka!" he shouted. "That's it! Follow me!" He led the family out onto the front porch, which was swarming with reporters and cameramen.

"Are you conceding the election?" one reporter asked.

"Are you giving up?" another reporter asked.

"That's what I just asked!" the first reporter said angrily.

"Oh, that's what 'concede' means?" The second reporter quickly opened up a dictionary app on his phone.

Ignoring them and speaking directly to the cameras, Mr. Armas declared, "We have found a way for Missy to take office."

"We have?" Missy whispered.

"After hours of scouring Article II, Section 1 of The Constitution, we've found that the age to take office as president is no younger than thirty-five..."

"Don't tell them that!" Dad interjected.

"I'm pretty sure they already know that, Dad. Isn't that the whole point?" Gloria said under her breath.

"I'm *conceiting*?" Missy asked.

"Concede, and no," Mr. Armas corrected. "Under the Twelfth Amendment, if the runner-up doesn't have enough votes to take office, then it becomes the responsibility of the House of Representatives to decide who becomes president, as happened in 1824 when the House voted to put John Quincy Adams into office. So you see, there *is* a precedent..."

Silence, as the reporters scribbled in their notebooks ferociously.

"What does that mean for Missy?" one reporter asked.

"It means," said Mr. Armas, beaming, "that we're going to Washington, D.C.!"

"All right!" said Missy, jumping up and down excitedly.

"No way!" said Mom. "I don't care how many reporters are standing in our front yard. I'm your mother, Missy, and you heard what I said before..."

"I sure did, Mom," Missy said reassuringly, "and I would never question your authority. But from what I recall, you said that I could never be president while I was under *that* roof. Now we're outside—so Washington, D.C., it is!"

"Now *that's* presidential problem-solving," a reporter declared, impressed.

"What can you say?" his colleague chimed in. "She's not a dope."

"Okay, fine," Mom said, sensing the tide turning against her on this one. "To Washington."

Missy high-fived Mr. Armas and gave her mom a huge bear hug, practically tackling her. "*Hooray!*"

CHAPTER 8

Missy, Mom, Dad, Gloria, and Mr. Armas exited the bus station in Washington, D.C., as fans and reporters snapped photos of them.

"Missy! Over here!" a teenage boy shouted.

"You go, girl!" a young woman called out to her.

"You go, too!" Missy responded. "Or stay. You choose!" Then she leaned over to Mr. Armas. "Was that a presidential thing to say?"

As they passed a nearby frozen yogurt store, the friendly owners waved at Missy.

"I love froyo!" Missy exclaimed.

"Well, how about a free cone on us?" the owner offered. "It would be an honor to serve a double scoop to our next president!"

"Free froyo?? Thanks!" Missy said happily, dashing into the shop.

A reporter standing nearby recorded a live segment. "This just in: Missy loves froyo!"

Moments later, at the busy New York Stock Exchange, a phone rang and a young stockbroker answered the call.

"What?" he said into the phone. "Missy loves froyo? Thanks for the tip." He hung up quickly, yelling to everyone who could hear: "Missy loves frozen yogurt! Get your hands on any froyo stocks and buy, *buy*, BUY!"

Back in Washington, D.C., Mr. Armas was showing Missy's family around the city as Gloria people-watched and Mom and Dad held hands. "And this is the National Mall," Mr. Armas said, stretching his arms out happily.

"I love malls!" Missy cried. "Build-a-Bear! American Girl! The Nike Store! The food court! Ooh, I hope they have Auntie Anne's!"

"Sorry, Missy, not that kind of mall," Mr. Armas said, chuckling. "The National Mall goes from the Capitol to the Lincoln Memorial and is bisected by our great Washington Monument."

"So it's a mall without a food court?" Missy asked, trying to piece it together.

"Not exactly. Why don't you and I take a little stroll together and I'll show you around a bit. Then we can go to the House," Mr. Armas said, winking at Missy's parents.

"Whose house are we going to anyway?" Missy asked, waving goodbye to her parents and skipping alongside Mr. Armas. "Should we bring cookies or something?"

"Not *someone's* house, no—the House of Representatives," Mr. Armas replied. "Do you know what they do there, Missy?"

"Right! They pass all the laws. I remember that from Mrs. Browning's class."

"Exactly. You'll be speaking to 435 voting members of the House today. That number proportionally represents the population of each of our fifty states. Do you remember the names of the U.S. territories?"

"Um, American Samoa, Guam, Puerto Rico, the U.S. Virgin Islands and... oh gosh, I know this, I know I know this... and uh... I give up."

"The Northern Mariana Islands."

"Shoot! I knew that one!"

At the National Museum of American History, Mr. Armas showed Missy a tattered, antique flag with fourteen stars. "This flag from the War of 1812 was the inspiration for our national anthem."

"*The Star-Spangled Banner*!" Missy said.

"Correct," Mr. Armas beamed.

Inside the Library of Congress, Missy gazed in wonder at the size of the domed roof. "This place is GI-NORMOUS!" she squealed, only to be shushed by several of the librarians and patrons at once. "Oops! Sorry!"

At the Martin Luther King, Jr. Memorial, Missy re-enacted MLK's most famous speech. "I have a dream!" she said proudly.

Standing next to the Lincoln Memorial, Missy recited his celebrated Gettysburg Address. "'Fourscore and seven years ago—'" she started. "Mr. Armas, how long *is* fourscore and seven years anyway?"

"Each score is twenty years," he replied.

Missy took a moment to do the math, using her fingers to count. "So that's... five, six, *eighty-seven* years! That's older than my grandma!"

At the Vietnam Veterans Memorial, Mr. Armas placed his hand over the name of his uncle, Ricardo Armas. Missy bowed her head in respect.

As Missy and Mr. Armas headed toward the Capitol Building, Missy tapped him on the shoulder. "Um, Mr. Armas, can I ask you something? It was really cool seeing everything today, but where are all the monuments for women?"

"That's an excellent question, Missy. The National Women's History Museum will be built right here." Mr. Armas pointed to a construction site that was nothing more than a hole in the ground.

"That's just a big dirt hole," Missy said, feeling disappointed. "Is there anything for girls that we can actually see? When I become president, I'll make sure this gets done quickly. All of these huge statues, and hardly any are of women. That needs to change!"

"I think you'll enjoy this next stop then," Mr. Armas smiled. He and Missy walked into the beautiful rotunda of the Capitol Building. Inside was a marble monument of Elizabeth Cady Stanton, Susan B. Anthony, and Lucretia Mott. Missy stood there for a while, admiring it.

"These three women fought hard for women's rights, Missy," Mr. Armas said. "They'd be so proud of you and the way you're making history. Are you ready for this?"

Missy puffed out her chest proudly as she walked up to the door of the House Chamber.

"Let's go kick some glass. Ceilings, that is."

CHAPTER 9

"The House will come to order," the Speaker said, banging the gavel again. "The House recognizes the gentleman from Indiana." The Indiana representative stood up.

"The votes have been tallied: twenty-eight votes for the runner-up, and 250,000,001 votes for Missy," he said matter-of-factly.

Young people all over the country were tuning in from their own devices to watch the action unfold.

At the home of the Indiana representative, his daughter, Anousheh, was watching live from her tablet with her friend David. "It's so cool that Missy's with your dad at work!" David exclaimed.

"I know! I can't wait for a girl president!" Anousheh beamed.

Across the country in California, twin girls watched from their laptop. "We love you, Missy!" they called out to the picture on the screen.

In Maine, Oregon, Florida, and every state in between, families logged on to the Internet to cheer Missy on.

But back at the House Chamber in Washington, D.C., things were in utter chaos. Cheers and boos alike echoed from the walls. Some representatives folded their arms angrily, murmuring their distaste, while others gave each other high fives, taking historic selfies to post online later. The Speaker banged his gavel.

"Quiet! Quiet on the floor! This is a highly unusual circumstance. We're faced with deciding who will become our next president: someone who received fewer than 0.1% of the votes... or a nine-year-old who received 99.9% of the votes. I honestly didn't think it was possible for this election to get any stranger, but, well—there you have it. Missy, would you like to say something?"

Missy stood up and cleared her throat as the cameras zoomed in on her. "Yessir, thank you," she said politely as she approached the podium.

"My dream is that in *onescore*... we can celebrate all the people who have made this country so awesome. Whether it's with monuments or statues or fully built museums—not just holes in the ground where a museum *might* go—or laws that better help and protect all people and their families. So many different kinds of people have dedicated their lives to this country. But you might not know that from walking around this city. Or from reading a history textbook. Or from watching the news. See, our country has an amazing history, but our *her*-story isn't quite as well-known.

"I just went for a stroll around the National Mall," Missy continued, "which is nothing like a mall at all—because a mall has lots of men's and *women's* mannequins everywhere... anyway, because many different people from all over helped us be here today, it's important that we continue to celebrate them and pass their knowledge on to younger generations. In conclusion, there should be equal statues for all... just like at the mall. Cool—that rhymed!"

"And this makes you fit to be president *why?*" the House Speaker challenged. But before Missy could answer, her mom bounced up from her seat.

"I'd like to say something, if you don't mind," Mom said.

"Actually, I do mind. Who are *you?*" the Speaker glowered.

"Missy's mother. You have a mother, don't you?" Mom stared the Speaker down.

Meanwhile, in a house across the country, an older woman watching C-SPAN from a rocking chair, petting a cat, glanced over at a photo of her son on the side table next to her. "You sure do, Bradley," the House Speaker's mom muttered.

The Speaker quickly took his seat and sat up straight. "Missy's mother has the floor!"

"Thank you," Mom said. "I was dead set against all this presidential business in the beginning, but the more I've seen in the past seventy-two hours, the more I've realized that Missy is exactly what this country needs: inspiration for the next generation of leaders—our children. We live in a country where young people are not only the most diverse they've ever been, but for the first time young people also represent the largest demographic of the American population. They'll have to live in this world longer than we will, so we should support their voices and hear what they have to say!"

The assembled Congress members grumbled.

"Listen to what kids say? That's ridiculous!" one shouted.

"Support the voices of children? Hogwash!" another agreed.

"Inspire a new generation of leaders? What for? So they can run against us and take our jobs away? Never!" declared a third.

The entire House of Representatives glared angrily at Missy's mother, who by this point had begun to sweat nervously.

"Uh, and we promise, as First Parents, that Missy will have a strict no-phones-at-the-dinner-table policy and no access to the White House or POTUS social media accounts until she's thirteen. Thank you," Mom said, turning as pale as a ghost and practically running back to her seat.

"If the mother of the candidate is finished, we can move on," the Speaker said, rising from his seat again. Missy's mom nodded quickly. "Okay. Let's vote."

Missy leaned over to Mr. Armas. "I'm done for," she said, putting her face in her hands.

Gloria saw this and came up with an idea. "Mom? Dad? Missy's in trouble and I can help. Well, me and the millions of kids of America. Can I have my phone back to help out my little sis? Just for a minute?

Mom and Dad couldn't help but be moved by Gloria's heartfelt concern over Missy. Mom took a sharp breath, hoping what she was about to do was for the best. "Gloria," Mom began. "That is really sweet of you. If you think you can actually rally some kids to help Missy by using your phone, then we'll help you."

Mom pulled Gloria's phone out of her purse. Gloria salivated in anticipation. But as she went to take her phone from Mom's hands, Dad snatched it first.

"But," Dad said, "we aren't giving this phone to you to stir up any more controversy. Responsible use only. Got it?"

"Mom, Dad, I got it. I should have asked permission before I recorded Missy. And I definitely should have thought twice before posting it to the Internet. These phones are awesome, but kind of tricky too. We can see the news—and we can also BE the news—with just one click. That's a lot of responsibility to carry around in your pocket. So don't worry. I've learned my lesson! No more posting without permission—ever!"

Mom and Dad nodded in agreement as Gloria accepted her phone—and the many responsibilities that come with it—back into her life.

"I won't let you down!" Gloria said to her parents, her little sister, and all the kids of America. She quickly typed....

CHAPTER 10

The Speaker banged his gavel again. "Now for the vote. Those who elect Missy President say—" But the Speaker didn't finish his sentence. He was interrupted by his phone's loud ringtone. "If you'll excuse me for a moment," he said, taking his phone out of his pocket. "A text message from my children." He opened the message, which read, "VOTE FOR MISSY OR ELSE, DAD. Luv u. Us."

He began to raise the gavel just as the Indiana representative's phone went off too. A message from Anousheh read, "Daddy, please, please vote Missy. She's the best girl for the job and you know it!"

Another Rep's phone went off and the message from her kids read, "Will clean room 4 Missy vote."

And another message, "Missy can do it! So can you! Vote!"

And another: "Don't be a dope!
Vote Missy! Plz?"

And another: "<3 u Mommy. Vote
Missy if u <3 me!"

And another: "#KidsMakeHerstory
need Dad's help!"

And another and another and another, until the phones of all the representatives were going off with messages from their kids, their constituents' kids, and kids all around the country, lobbying them to vote for Missy.

Gloria smiled proudly in her seat.

"Gloria, did *you* do this?" Dad asked, leaning over.

"A girl never tells her secrets," Gloria said. "But yeah, I guess I did."

The Speaker banged his gavel so furiously that it broke against the podium. "Quiet! Quiet, *please*! Everybody turn off your phones and get it together. We need to vote! Those who elect Missy President, please say aye!"

Missy crossed her fingers and toes. Mr. Armas closed his eyes tightly. Mom and Dad held hands, while kids around the country sat on the edges of their seats.

"Aye!" one voice shouted from the back of the room.

"Aye!" chimed in another.

"AYE!" "AYE!" "AYE!" Hundreds of voices echoed the affirmative vote.

"Those opposed?" the Speaker asked. Somewhere in the far distance, a pin dropped. "Well, then, the ayes have it. Missy, welcome to the White House. Looks like we'll be working together. I hope you're ready for it."

The House Chamber exploded in a giant celebration.

Red, white, and blue balloons fell from the ceiling; cameramen hugged reporters; reporters hugged members of Congress.

Mom, Dad, and Gloria stood watching from the balcony in awe. Somewhere in Indiana, David and Anousheh high-fived, and the twin teenage girls in California cheered with joy.

"We did it!" Missy said, jumping from her seat. "OMG!"

"*You* did it," Mr. Armas said. "I'm so proud of you."

"I couldn't have done it without you. That's why I'd like you to be my vice president, Mr. Armas," Missy said.

"Vice president? Are you sure, Missy?"

"Absolutely. You're the smartest person I know, and I'll need your help running the very best, most awesome country in the world," Missy answered, giving Mr. Armas a great big bear hug.

Around the nation, from New York City on the East Coast to San Diego on the West Coast, people celebrated Missy President.

"Kid power!" was the chant that could be heard from every neighborhood. A Missy President float led a Mardi Gras style parade in New Orleans. A boyfriend took a picture of his girlfriend at Mount Rushmore, and then used Photoshop to add a picture of Missy to the four men on the mountain. Kids watched C-SPAN on a giant screen at preschool and threw their juice boxes in the air.

"Kids can do anything!" they shouted.

"I am not a dope!"

Even in Buckingham Palace, Queen Elizabeth, wearing a bathrobe and crown over pink curlers, watched Missy become president. "About bloody time," she said, powering her laptop down.

Back in Washington, D.C., the Speaker came up to shake Missy's hand. "Your first duty as president will be to pick your cabinet. Let me know if I can be of service."

"My *cabinet?*" Missy's eyes lit up. "Well, I saw a super-cool monkey-shaped one at Ikea. Dad, can we go get it this weekend?"

Mr. Armas laughed. "This is sure going to be fun!"

"I better call some friends back at school and tell them to get ready. I have a whole staff to fill!" Missy said, immediately getting down to business. "Mom, Dad, can I borrow your phone? Or better yet, now that I'm president, maybe I can get a phone of my own, pretty please? I need to call Jonah and Lily and Max and Jackie and Jackson and tell them that I need them for my presidential staff, pronto!"

The Indiana representative came over to speak with Missy. "Sorry to interrupt," he said, "but I just wanted to congratulate you on a race well won. I have a very smart, wonderful daughter at home just like you. Her name is Anousheh. I bet the two of you would get along just swimmingly."

"I'm not much of a swimmer, but I'd love to meet her!" Missy gushed. "In fact, Mr. Armas told me that I need to appoint a "secret-ary" of State. Is she good at keeping secrets?"

"The best," the Indiana representative chuckled. "I look forward to working with you, Missy."

"Just you wait, America. Missy is here to help! But I can't do it alone! Whether you're two or 102, I want the very, very best Americans on my presidential staff!"

"Business can wait until tomorrow," Mr. Armas said, leading Missy back to her family.

Gloria tugged on Missy's sleeve. "Hey sis, I posted that video to be funny. I'm sorry. I hope you're not mad at me."

"You clearly have a knack for publicity and online communication, Glor. I just hope next time you'll ask permission before you post something private online."

"Can I post this?" Gloria threw her arms around Missy, and raised her camera high for a selfie.

The sisters yelled, "GO MISSY!" into the camera then broke into a fit of laughter.

TO BE CONTINUED...

Randi Zuckerberg is a professional technologist and an amateur mom. She is extremely passionate about encouraging women and girls to take on bigger roles in business, leadership, and entrepreneurship, and feels that media and pop culture are the best way to spread this message. In 2012, Randi started Zuckerberg Media with the mission of creating meaningful media projects to support this goal. If you liked this book, come party with Randi on Sprout with *Dot.*, her animated children's TV show about a tech--savvy girl and friends, or listen to her weekly business show, *Dot Complicated*, on SiriusXM channel 111. Randi has a B.A. from Harvard University and lives in NYC with her husband, Brent, and sons Asher and Simcha.

Natasha Lewin is a civil and human rights activist, first, and an award-winning writer second. She resides in Los Angeles.

Joan Coleman is an artist and illustrator specializing in book illustration, apparel and graphic design. Visit Joan at www.InkWonderland.com

★ Social Media Ballot ★

My name is:

I am running for President of the United States because:

My key issues are:

My running mate is:

You should vote for me because:

Snap a photo of your answers or shoot a video (with your parents' permission of course!) and tell us what YOU would do if you were president. Ask your parents to email us your responses to electme@missypresident.com or post to their social media accounts using #MissyPresident!

www.missypresident.com

★ Discussion Questions ★

1. Do you think it was wrong of Gloria to post the video without Missy's permission? What would you do if someone posted something of you without your consent?

2. What were the unexpected consequences of Gloria's decision to post the video?

3. Was the media correct in jumping on the 'Missy President' story because it was newsworthy? Should the media have been more protective of Missy's privacy?

4. What do you think of Gloria's comment about how technology is changing world events, especially as it relates to government? Do you agree or disagree?

5. Who would you like to see a statue of in Washington D.C. and why?

6. How can parents and children have a more open discussion about technology?

7. What is appropriate tech use at home or at the dinner table?

8. In the future, are we going to have to assume everything will be public and on the Internet at all times? If so, would that change the way you live your life?

9. At the end of the book, the children of America help to elect Missy. Do you think political issues could be resolved if more young people banded together? Which issues might America's youth help resolve?

10. What should be Missy's first act as president?

COMING SOON
Book Two of Missy President

A lot can happen between Election Day and Missy's inauguration...

Will the nation still rally around a nine-year-old president in January? Or will there be a recount of the votes?

Which friends will Missy invite to become members of her Cabinet? Will Gloria have a role to play? Or will she be left out? And will Missy encourage other kids around the world to start a movement of kid politicians?

What will Missy's inauguration look like? Who will perform? What will it be like for Missy's family to move in to the White House?

What will be Missy's first order of business as president? Will she have a code name with the Secret Service? How many grilled cheeses can the White House Chef make in a single day? And will Trog be the nation's First Frog?

All this and much, much more in the next installment of Missy President, due out in January 2017!

Made in the USA
Lexington, KY
06 March 2017